Midnight Madness

Wesley and Anna haven't seen each other since they both quit high school years ago. Their reasons for quitting were as different as they were, or so it might seem, until they discover plenty they never knew about each other in the bed department of Bloom's furniture store.

"A gentle little comedy…a play that will delight and touch audiences for years to come."

Toronto Star

Nicola Cavendish as Anna and Tom McCamus as Wesley in the Arts Club Seymour Street Stage production. Photo by Glen Erikson.

Midnight Madness

Dave Carley

THE SUMMERHILL SEASON

The Summerhill Season is published by:
Summerhill Press Ltd., 52 Shaftesbury Avenue
Toronto, Ontario M4T 1A2

Distributed by:
University of Toronto Press, 5201 Dufferin Street
Downsview, Ontario M3H 5T8

General Editor: Michelle Maynes
Cover illustration: John Etheridge
Author photo: Nir Bareket
Printed and bound in Canada by Metropole Litho Inc.

Canadian Cataloguing in Publication Data

Carley, Dave, 1955
Midnight Madness

(The Summerhill Season)
A play.
ISBN 0-920197-88-4

I. Title. II. Series.

PS 8555.A7397M5 1989   C812'.54   C89-095181-0
PR9199.3.C37M5 1989

Enquiries regarding production rights should be directed to
Patricia Ney, Christopher Banks and Associates, 219 Dufferin Street,
Ste 305, Toronto, Ontario M6K 1Y9. Phone: (416) 530-4002.

Running time is 85 minutes.

For Mig

Midnight Madness premiered on August 11, 1988, at the Gravenhurst Opera House, Gravenhurst, Ontario, as a co-production of the Muskoka Festival and Arbor Theatre. The cast was as follows:

WESLEY: John Dolan

ANNA: Michelle Fisk

MR. BLOOM: Graham Greene

Director: Bill Glassco

Assistant Director: Michael Shamata

Set and Costume Design: Myles Warren

Lighting Design: Andrew Rabbets

Sound Design: Evan B. Turner

The play was re-staged by Michael Shamata with the same cast and opened at Toronto's Tarragon Theatre on October 18, 1988

Acknowledgments

The creation of *Midnight Madness*
was generously assisted by the Ontario
Arts Council. A workshop was
conducted at the Muskoka Festival in
the summer of 1987, directed by
Bill Glassco, with John Dolan as Wesley
and Michelle Fisk as Anna.

The author would like to thank
Bill Glassco, John Dolan and
Michelle Fisk; and also Michael Ayoub,
Jennifer Dean, Graham Greene,
Glenda MacFarlane, Kevin McGugan,
Patricia Ney, Judith Rudakoff,
Michael Shamata, Myles Warren and
Helen Weinzweig.

Characters

WESLEY Marshall, about 32

ANNA Bregner, the same age

The voice of Mr. BLOOM, about 75

The Setting

The second floor Bed Department of Bloom's Furniture, a run-down store on the main street of Ashburnham (pronounced Ash-burn'm), a small city in Ontario.

Offstage is the Lighting Department, identifiable by a glow. Everything in the Bed Department is marked down, including a cannonball bed, a fairly rococo brass number and a large waterbed unit. There is some terrible art on the walls — large seascapes and stags in mountain glens.

The time is 1985

Note

Mr. Bloom does *not* speak with a heavy Jewish accent. Such an accent is completely inappropriate for a man who has lived his entire life in a small Ontario city.

The play begins in darkness. BLOOM's *voice is heard over the intercom speaker;* WESLEY's *is not.*

BLOOM: Wesley. Try again.

WESLEY: OK, how's this. "One old Jew. One young Presbyterian. Two men, a hundred and eight years of accumulated guilt."

BLOOM: I don't like that word guilt. It makes me nervous.

WESLEY: But wait — I'm going to tie it in with selling the bed. "These men understand sin. They know all about crimes of passion. They can sell you the weapon —

> (*Lights up.* WESLEY *is on the waterbed, holding the intercom mike in one hand, a styrofoam cup of sherry in the other*)

— The revolutionary Waterbed Home Entertainment Centre, complete with stereo headboard, climate control and The Undulation Feature.

9

Motion below to match the motion above.
Friends, customers. Come to Bloom's and invest
in some liquid guilt."

BLOOM: (*enjoying himself*) Too racy. And the religious
stuff still makes me nervous. But it shows prom-
ise. You should go into advertising after tomorrow.

WESLEY: Yeah, yeah.

BLOOM: You know hundreds of fancy words, you
could sell all sorts of things.

WESLEY: I haven't unloaded this waterbed have I. And
we've only got one day left. Jeez sir — I haven't
had a customer in an hour.

BLOOM: You think it's a mob scene down here?

WESLEY: This Midnight Madness idea — I don't know.
It just isn't the hour for buying furniture. This is
the hour of marital duty.

BLOOM: It's nearly midnight! They got that done by
nine-thirty. Think of some more funny ads.

WESLEY: Why don't we close for the night.

BLOOM: The sign says we're open to midnight, so we
stay open. Do that Marxist one again, I liked it.
"Rise up couch potatoes of the world." Come on,
humour an old man.

WESLEY: I'm gonna miss this old place.

BLOOM: No mush my son.

WESLEY: This isn't mush, this is reality. I've got pre-partum depression.

BLOOM: You should talk normal, you could get a girl. And save the emotion for tomorrow. Mrs. B's making us a cake, I've got some nice wine, we'll drink this store out in style. Tomorrow. But it's still today, we've got time on our hands and, if you don't want to make up ads, you should go —

WESLEY: (*over*) Dust.

BLOOM: — dust. If the legs worked better I'd be up there in a flash and I bet if I ran my finger down the headboard of your precious stereo waterbed I'd find — dust.

WESLEY: (*rubbing sleeve over headboard*) Clean as a baby's bum.

BLOOM: Fifty years, I've never had an employee who dusted. Not a one. (*pause*) For heaven's sake, there's someone coming in the door! Customer alert. (*voice fading a bit as he approaches the customer; intercom was left on*) Hello young lady.

ANNA: Hi.

BLOOM: Lovely evening isn't it. What can I do you for?

ANNA: Is the Bed Department still upstairs?

BLOOM: Oh yes, it's this way — the stairs are behind the clocks there. Watch the last step dear. (*over intercom*) Snap to it Wes, maybe you can unload the waterbed.

> (WESLEY *has leapt into action, dusting a headboard or two, straightening a bed-spread, adjusting his tie. It's a fairly co-ordinated, practised sequence, which he completes by flipping on the muzak*)

> (ANNA *enters, frowning back at the step. She sees* WESLEY, *and smiles*)

WESLEY: Hi. May I help you.

ANNA: You could start by fixing that step. I nearly killed myself.

WESLEY: It's even worse going down.

ANNA: A little gnome told me the beds were here.

WESLEY: And did he tell you it's all on sale?

ANNA: I saw the ad in the *Examiner*.

WESLEY: Cash or cheque. Coloured beads. Wampum. Just no credit. (*pause*) I know you.

ANNA: Those are the three scariest words in the language.

WESLEY: We went to Ashburnham High together.

ANNA: Stinky Harrison!!

WESLEY: No. Wesley Marshall.

ANNA: Wesley Marshall — Jude's brother! You've changed!

WESLEY: I'm less blemished. You're Anna Bregner.

ANNA: I'm flattered you recognize me.

WESLEY: You haven't changed a bit, hardly.

ANNA: Wesley Marshall.

WESLEY: Yeah.

ANNA: I haven't seen you since high school. How many years is that —

WESLEY: — Fourteen.

ANNA: God. Your sister and I were best friends for — weeks. We did everything together, then she stole Billy Dingle from me.

WESLEY: They got married.

ANNA: Yeah, I heard. Well, isn't this something! What're you doing here, anyway.

WESLEY: I'm second floor manager. For one more day. Then we're retail history.

ANNA: I can't imagine downtown without Bloom's. (*points to cannonball*) The cannonball's nice.

WESLEY: Solid pine.

ANNA: Made in Canada?

WESLEY: I think it's assembled here. The wood might be ours.

BLOOM: (*intercom*) Welcome to Bloom's Midnight Madness Sale. For the next ten minutes everything is 10 percent off the last 25 percent off. Especially beds and lighting.

ANNA: Is that Bloom?

WESLEY: Yup.

ANNA: He's cute.

WESLEY: Cute?

ANNA: Sweet.

WESLEY: Bloom! He's grumpy, nosey, bossy…

ANNA: I don't believe you.

WESLEY: Believe me.

ANNA: How long have you worked for him then?

WESLEY: Just a decade.

ANNA: Ten years!

WESLEY: Why not? I'm fond of the old guy.

ANNA: Apparently. (*of the muzak*) And you've listened to that muzak the whole time?

WESLEY: Awful eh. Just a sec and I'll put on something better. (*turns off muzak, mucks about for cassette tapes*)

ANNA: (*of the brass bed*) These things always remind me of Bob Dylan.

WESLEY: You want some Bob Dylan?

ANNA: No, I said this bed reminds me of him. "Lay lady, lay…"

WESLEY: I thought you wanted Dylan. I haven't got much new stuff. Post-1900. Hey — do you remember Miss Eaton's English class, how she'd pull apart the lyrics to songs? She always said it should be "Lie Lady, Lie".

ANNA: Miss Eaton reminded me of a chipping sparrow on acid.

WESLEY: I never thought of her that way, but you're right. And that other song, with the line, "Ain't no one for to give you no pain." Triple negative, it used to drive her around the bend. Billy'd whistle it at the back. (*distracted from putting tape on*) You were front corner by the door. Till Christmas —

ANNA: — You have quite the memory. So tell me, why should I buy a brass bed?

WESLEY: Beats me. I hate 'em. I've been trying to keep them out of the department but the minute I sell one Bloom whips off and orders another. Drives me crazy. They're hell for getting fingerprints — one grubby kid can cost me fifteen minutes polishing. The cannonball just needs the odd shot of Pledge. (*notices* ANNA *staring at him*) Is something wrong?

ANNA: What. Oh, sorry. (*points to waterbed*) Hoo — is that a waterbed!?

WESLEY: Somewhat in the ritzy bracket.

ANNA: I'll say.

WESLEY: This baby and I have been together three years. I can't sell it to save my life and Bloom never lets me forget it. It's got a stereo, digital alarm... it undulates at the flick of a switch. (*flips switch, nothing happens*) It's supposed to undulate.

ANNA: (*sitting on it*) What do you call this?

WESLEY: No no, there's a little wave-maker inside. (*kicks bed*) It's like a mini-waterpark. C'mon baby—

BLOOM: How's everything up there?

WESLEY: (*to* ANNA) He's already bored silly —

BLOOM: — Wesley — can you hear me?

WESLEY: (*going to intercom*) I don't know how he's going to handle retirement. (*intercom*) Everything's copascetic.

BLOOM: That's a revolting word. I wouldn't say that to my worst enemy. I just wanted to tell you there are a couple of parties interested in the waterbed. They'll undoubtedly want to buy it, tomorrow. Do you catch my drift?

WESLEY: (*to* ANNA, *hand over mike*) He's using psychology on you. (*intercom*) She seems to favour the cannonball.

BLOOM: — And who can blame her, the cannonball's a lovely bed. But I'd feel *guilty* if I didn't warn her the waterbed's getting snapped up.

WESLEY: Roger sir.

ANNA: (*as* WESLEY *hangs up intercom*) Now tell me he's not cute. (*going to brass bed*) So you're really against brass beds eh.

WESLEY: It's just the fingerprints. Plus if you like to sit up and read the headframe freezes your back to death.

ANNA: They make me nostalgic. This one doesn't quite make it though. Don't you have anything more traditional?

WESLEY: Just what you see.

ANNA: So, tell me about the Dingles. How's married life treating them?

WESLEY: Not very well. They're divorced.

ANNA: Don't tell me — I can guess. Billy was having affairs of the heart.

WESLEY: You're about a foot off.

ANNA: I'm not surprised. Billy was born sleazy. All the time I was going with him he was sneaking around with your sister. (*tragic*) The milkshakes he was buying her. The peppermint Dentyne they were passing from mouth to mouth.

WESLEY: He was a creep deluxe. It was terrible for Jude.

ANNA: What's she doing now?

WESLEY: She's down in Toronto, working in computers.

ANNA: Who isn't.

WESLEY: Me.

ANNA: And me.

WESLEY: I mean, I.

ANNA: And I. See — some of Miss Eaton sunk in.
(*pause*) You know, if you keep kicking that thing
it'll spring a leak.

WESLEY: I want to make it undulate for you.

ANNA: It's OK. I'm not the waterbed type anyway.

WESLEY: What do you have now?

ANNA: A futon.

WESLEY: We never carried them. Mr. Bloom thinks
they're a fad.

ANNA: (*of waterbed*) And those aren't?

WESLEY: He owns the store.

ANNA: (*sighing, on brass bed*) This is heaven. You know
how you're not supposed to shop on an empty
stomach because when you hit the frozen cakes
you'll blow the budget? Well, I'm bone tired. I
want this one, now.

WESLEY: Really?

ANNA: On condition I don't have to move for twenty-
four hours. I got back to town three days ago and
I haven't stopped working. I'm staying at Mom's
but I've rented a place of my own and I spent all
yesterday and today painting. It's a dump but it's

in my son's school district, so he won't have to readjust. I mean, he's going to have to adjust to me, but this way his chums can stay the same.

WESLEY: What's his name?

ANNA: Jason.

WESLEY: Jason.

ANNA: And I know what you're thinking.

WESLEY: I'm not thinking anything!

ANNA: *My* Jason was the first. *I* pioneered the name. It's not my fault four billion Jason Josh Joels followed mine. Anyway, the kid's been living with Mom while I've been at school. But she's seventy now and Jason's on the cusp of puberty — I cannot sentence my mother, in her golden years, to that.

WESLEY: You'd think it would get easier the older he gets.

ANNA: Shows what you know. That boy's chock-full of hormones. His insides are like a microwave on full blast and he's about to blow the door off. (*makes a boom noise*)

WESLEY: Holy.

ANNA: Aw, he's a good kid but I'm beat. I'm going to get the apartment in operation this weekend, then next week I'll set up an office and get some currency. So I can pay for this bed. Did I tell you I'm a lawyer?

WESLEY: Your graduation notice was in the paper — congratulations!

ANNA: Thanks. Mom placed it. It's good publicity, I guess. You wouldn't believe how proud she is.

WESLEY: You're the first lawyer from our year.

ANNA: "Our year?"

WESLEY: Class of '71.

ANNA: I didn't quite graduate.

WESLEY: Neither did I, but it seemed like our year.

ANNA: (*sighs*) I painted ten hours yesterday and another eight today. (*relaxing on bed*) Do you mind?

WESLEY: Be my guest. There aren't any customers and Bloom can't get up the stairs anymore.

ANNA: What's over there?

WESLEY: The Lighting Department. I'm sort of in charge of it now too, but it's a disaster area. Bloom has this thing for swag lamps. The room's a jungle of dangling wires. You could get strangled, no probs.

ANNA: How do you know I'm the only lawyer?

WESLEY: I don't, not for sure, but I know what most
people are doing, from the paper, or sometimes
they come in here. You hear. Birth announce-
ments. They're all popping babies.

ANNA: I went to the reunion, to network. You weren't
there.

WESLEY: That's because I didn't go. Technically we
weren't eligible.

ANNA: Now you're the one being legalistic. Nobody
challenged me. They stamped my hand and in I
went, suffering a very bad case of *déja vu*.

WESLEY: I borrowed the neighbour's dog so I'd have
an excuse to walk by the school. If Jude had come
home I might've gone with her, but she figured
Billy'd be there, so she stayed clear.

ANNA: He's fat.

WESLEY: Billy!

ANNA: (*gesturing fatness*) Humungus!

WESLEY: Excellent!

ANNA: They're all fat.

WESLEY: The *Examiner* had a big write-up. I keep a
scrapbook.

ANNA: You do.

John Dolan as Wesley and Michelle Fisk as Anna in the Tarragon Theatre production. Photo by Michael Cooper

WESLEY: Yeah. Stupid huh.

ANNA: You're kind of a bear for punishment.

WESLEY: It's interesting to see how people's lives unfold. Some I could've predicted. Others are surprises.

ANNA: Anyone famous yet?

WESLEY: I did a TV commercial once in a grass skirt. No, nobody's famous. There are two doctors though: Anne McAdam and Walter Robey —

ANNA: — And Mary Lou Winters married one. How many d'you figure still live here?

WESLEY: No more than twenty-five.

ANNA: That's not many. I'll send 'em business cards.

WESLEY: Jim Schull died in a car accident.

ANNA: You're kidding. Which was he?

WESLEY: Short guy, Coke bottle glasses?

ANNA: I can't picture him. Any family?

WESLEY: A wife, two kids.

ANNA: That's really sad. Did you know him?

WESLEY: Not really, but I still felt bad. (*as* ANNA *pulls a thread off his jacket*) He never did anything against me. What're you doing?

ANNA: Sorry — it's the mother in me. You had a thread the size of a shoelace. Here's another one. (*distracted, points to cannonball*) Is this a queen?

WESLEY: Yes. We had it in one-and-a-half, but it sold yesterday.

ANNA: What time is it?

WESLEY: A quarter to.

ANNA: You close at midnight?

WESLEY: Midnight Madness. The clock's ticking and we're crazy for value.

ANNA: So I have fifteen minutes to choose. If I buy something tonight, will you deliver it tomorrow?

WESLEY: Pas doo problem.

ANNA: I'm climbing the walls at Mom's. She's in the Citi-Centre high-rise and I have to share a bedroom with Jason. Don't ever let anyone tell you thirteen year-olds can't snore. (*surveys room*) Decisions, decisions. I'd be a real hit with Jace if I got the waterbed.

WESLEY: I thought it was *your* bed —

ANNA: Oh it is, but Jason's at that age where it's important for his mom to look cool. His buddies have been coming round to inspect me. Mom's apartment was the gang's drop-in centre and the grade seven mafia's worried about the new regime.

WESLEY: (*kicking bed discreetly*) Should they worry?

ANNA: In my less tired moments I think my house'll be a haven for them all. We'll sit around at night and make popcorn and I'll get my guitar out and teach them old Joni Mitchell songs. They'll be having so much fun they'll never haunt another plaza. That's when I'm rested. Right now I think if just one of those fuzzy-lipped brats puts a sneaker over my threshold he'll never live to see grade eight.

WESLEY: (*a smile*) Jason sounds like a lucky kid.

ANNA: Aw — we get along. (*pause*) That's too bad about Jude and Billy — I'm sorry they split.

WESLEY: Don't be. I wasn't.

ANNA: There's something about them being divorced that offends my concept of rightness. They looked so good together. All that blondness. All those teeth. They were so cool.

WESLEY: But you were "in".

ANNA: Like Flynn, till I fell from grace. High school wasn't meant for you and me.

WESLEY: I know. We're the ones who blossom in later life. Every movie that's made on the subject has the high school heroes bombing out. Billy gets fat and you and I get to be president every time.

ANNA: That's lovely on celluloid — explain Mary Lou Winters.

WESLEY: Yeah.

ANNA: Rich and popular then, even more so now. I sweat my way through law school, she marries the doctor and gets to lounge around Forest Heights the rest of her life. Where's the justice.

WESLEY: She's miserable?

ANNA: Naw. She's happy as a clam. You should've seen her at the reunion. She was standing in the middle of the main hall and you could barely squeeze around her, the fur coat was that bulky. And attached to the mink was a very handsome doctor.

WESLEY: Did she recognize you?

ANNA: Immediately. "Which graduating class are you here with?" asked the dirty you-know-what. Well, we chatted for a few minutes — she never did introduce her doctor — and she made it very clear her behind was thoroughly in the butter. "And what about you dear?" she asked finally, as if she cared. Guess what I did. I'd had cards printed up and I handed her one. "Mary Lou," I said. "I'm a lawyer now. I do divorce work. Call me when Sawbones here dumps you."

WESLEY: Excellent!

ANNA: Oh God did it feel good. I turned around and whipped off and the triumph lasted oh ten feet, until I remembered Mary Lou was going home to a mansion in Forest Heights and crawling into bed with a gorgeous doctor, whereas I... (*shakes head*)

WESLEY: But you scored the telling blow.

ANNA: Not really. Mary Lou yelled after me, "I heard that line on TV!"

WESLEY: Yelled?

ANNA: Like a goddamn foghorn. Once a cheerleader, always a cheerleader. You could've heard her in the science wing. (*pause; of the brass bed*) I think I'll go with the brass.

WESLEY: I'd take the cannonball if I —

ANNA: — I like brass. OK OK I'll sleep on it. (*elbows* WESLEY) That's a Bed Department joke. Hey — what kind of salesman are you anyway, telling me not to buy something. How've you lasted a decade in sales?

WESLEY: Longer than that even. I've been here ten years and before that I was at Sears. Four years. Garden Supplies, so I'm up on my hoses too.

ANNA: Are you on commission?

WESLEY: Partly. It's not much of a living. I mean, you hear what a real estate agent makes in a good year — you have to wonder.

ANNA: It's unusual to work so long in one place.

WESLEY: It never occurred to me to leave. That's not true — I decided once I'd go back to school so I could get into computers like Jude but cripes — I can barely plug in a toaster. When a three-prong plug is hi-tech… (*shakes head*)

ANNA: What part of town do you live in?

WESLEY: East City, just below the hill. Same place as always.

ANNA: You still live at home?

WESLEY: Sort of. It's mine now. Mom died a year ago.

ANNA: I'm sorry.

WESLEY: And Dad died when I was eight.

ANNA: You have a whole house…

WESLEY: Yeah, I'm an orphan.

ANNA: I'd kill for a whole house. You wanna marry me?

WESLEY: It's actually not a big house.

> (*They laugh*)

ANNA: Aw darn, rejected again. Do you see Jude often?

WESLEY: Not really. We still phone on Sundays and she comes down for Christmas and Easter, but that's about it. I'll tell her you're back in town. She's still curious about what everyone's doing. You should've heard her when she found out Mary Lou Winters was living up in Forest Heights. "That bitch climbed that hill on her back!" Sorry.

ANNA: Jude always had a way with words.

WESLEY: Anyway, that's about it for me. It's kind of embarrassing there's so little to tell.

ANNA: Better too little than too much.

WESLEY: I don't know. Sometimes I feel like I've spent fifteen years sort of treading water. You know, Wesley sold beds but Jesus fed crowds.

BLOOM: Attention shoppers. Bloom's Furniture is going to close for the evening. All shoppers should hurry up and buy what she wants. (*pause*) Is everything OK Wesley?

WESLEY: (*to* ANNA) I told you I was an orphan? (*intercom*) Yes sir. Everything's fine.

BLOOM: And is that discerning young lady still admiring our beds?

WESLEY: Yes sir.

BLOOM: There may be some salient factors about those beds you've forgotten to mention.

WESLEY: Such as?

BLOOM: Perhaps you could come downstairs for a moment please.

WESLEY: But Mr. Bloom...

BLOOM: "To obey is better than sacrifice; and to hearken than the fat of rams." Get the hell down here.

WESLEY: (*to* ANNA) I'll just be a sec. Maybe you'd like to pick out a lamp. I could throw in a swag with the cannonball — (*intercom*) I'm on my way.

> (WESLEY *leaves, remembers that intercom speaker is still on, returns and switches it off.* ANNA *pokes about; she can kick the waterbed, primp for a second in front of a mirror, and look in the swag room. Finally she switches the intercom speaker button to* "receive")

BLOOM: Tell her you'll give her the waterbed for 50 percent.

WESLEY: She doesn't want it.

BLOOM: Throw in some art. We have to get rid of the damn thing.

WESLEY: Take it home for Mrs. Bloom.

BLOOM: She gets motion sick from taking a bath. What'm I going to do with a waterbed left over?

WESLEY: It won't undulate. Anyway, she's nibbling at the cannonball.

BLOOM: That, I can unload at my brother's store. The waterbed calls for a sucker.

WESLEY: She's way too smart.

BLOOM: At 50 percent even a professor can't resist.

WESLEY: But sir.

BLOOM: Try. For me. For Bloom's. Once more into the breach. Once more round the mulberry bush. See. I can talk like you. A waterbed for posterity.

ANNA: (*picking up mike*) Beds to Bloom. Beds to Bloom. I don't care how cute you are, I'm not shelling out for plastic-wrapped water.

BLOOM: Don't be hasty.

ANNA: This is taste, not haste.

WESLEY: Anna — think. What Jesus walked on, you can sleep on.

BLOOM: (*reproving*) Wesley! (*to* ANNA) Young lady, 50 percent off.

ANNA: You add a dozen disciples I'll consider it a deal. Which reminds me — will you send the stallion back up?

BLOOM: Stallion?

ANNA: The guy in the sweater.

BLOOM: (*long pause*) Wesley?

ANNA: That's the man. (*another tone*) While I've got you on the line, Mr. Bloom, you want to explain that room full of swag lamps?

BLOOM: What about them.

ANNA: Who buys 'em?

BLOOM: Citizens.

ANNA: Of what planet?

BLOOM: Ashburnham. There's a vast market for swag lamps.

ANNA: Wesley worries about strangulation.

BLOOM: Wesley worries for recreation.

(WESLEY *has entered and he reaches for the
intercom.* ANNA *hands it over after a second's tease*)

WESLEY: You've got the nerve of a canal horse.

ANNA: (*laughing*) Sorry — I couldn't resist.

WESLEY: This is a store you know; we have an image of
professionalism to maintain. (*beginning to laugh*)
It's not funny. OK. It's mildly amusing.

BLOOM: What's going on up there?

WESLEY: Stallion! What's he gonna think! You're really
terrible. (*over intercom*) Sir: the customer has been
apprehended. I've got her tied to the cannonball.

BLOOM: Wesley. You shouldn't even joke like that.

ANNA: I just love the way he talks.

BLOOM: I'm locking up now. You could shoot a can-
non down George Street.

WESLEY: Want some help with the cash?

BLOOM: What cash? Will you see the young lady out,
whenever.

WESLEY: Yes sir.

BLOOM: Bless you son.

WESLEY: (*putting down the mike*) He sounded tired,
didn't he.

ANNA: It must be really draining on him. This place is an institution.

WESLEY: It had to happen. Bloom's survived for fifty years, but now…

ANNA: There's nobody to carry on?

WESLEY: One son, Jay, is a doctor in Texas and Ronny's a lawyer. We thought Ronny would take over — he used to work here summers — but Bloom didn't want him in retail, and apparently he's doing well in Toronto. Bloom's lonely. His wife isn't much company, she's busy with this and that, and he's got boo-all except the store.

ANNA: It's sad.

WESLEY: It's different for me because I'll get another job. He's going to retire and rot. I don't know how he'll stand coming downtown even, because he'll see this place sitting here, a big empty hulk… Anyway, we're having a farewell bash. Nothing major. Just me, the Blooms, the part-timers, assorted spouses. Ronny's coming back and, for a surprise, I've invited all the retired employees I could trace. We're going to have some of Bloom's home-made hooch, crank up the muzak and have a big pajama party. If there are any beds left.

ANNA: Isn't anybody buying the building?

WESLEY: It's a white elephant. Maybe they'll make it a bingo hall. The only things that survive down here anymore are the specialty boutiques. Eaton's vamoosed to the mall, so did Woolworth's.

ANNA: And the supermarket's gone! I went there today and —

WESLEY: — They couldn't get extra parking. Someday you'll drive down George Street and there'll be this giant cobweb strung across the road. I'm under no illusions. I've gone out to the malls and strolled around the furniture stores. They feel cleaner. They have air conditioning that works. They have better stuff.

ANNA: Yeah, you have to admit, some of this stuff is pretty godawful.

WESLEY: It's not that bad!

ANNA: The Hall of Swag?

WESLEY: Yeah. But those malls — they ain't Bloom's. There's only one Bloom's. There's something to be said for those stairs you climbed —

ANNA: Dangerous?

WESLEY: And worn into curves by fifty years of shoppers. Look at that ceiling!

ANNA: Pressed tin.

WESLEY: When did you last see that? In the office
there's a whole wall of family portraits —
Bloom's parents and his family, a photo of the
town in Russia they came from... Ah, I don't
know, we've been done in by the chains. I know
it's evolution, the fittest survive and all that but
there's still nothing wrong with mourning a store
like this — nobody's going to cry when a chain
dies. They just get bigger and more anonymous,
the cash they rake in flows out of town and when
the money dries up they leave and nobody gives
a damn. It all started with Kentucky Fried
Chicken.

ANNA: (*pause*) Do you think it's kind of for the better?

WESLEY: What do you mean.

ANNA: For you.

WESLEY: (*wary*) Why.

ANNA: To get out of here.

WESLEY: Why.

ANNA: Because —

WESLEY: Since when is losing your job "kind of for the
better"?

ANNA: It'll you know, push you out, into the real
world.

WESLEY: Why the hell does everyone think this place isn't real? You and Jude — you're a pair. This place may be dying but it's real enough. It's a lot more real than some plastic damn mall. If that's what you think is real then I don't know what the hell you're doing here.

ANNA: Getting a bargain from a grouchy salesman?

WESLEY: Get your bargains at Nutty Normans. Go buy your bed there. Then you can rest assured you could get the same deal coast to coast, that oughta make it a touch more real for you. I mean, if something's real once, you repeat it a thousand times it must be even more so.

ANNA: Wait a second.

WESLEY: I'm sick of people telling me —

ANNA: — Wes! Wes. I want a bed, I just want to buy a bed. All right?

WESLEY: Sorry.

ANNA: It's OK.

WESLEY: I don't normally chew out customers. I'm really tired I guess.

ANNA: That makes two of us. I'll buy a bed and take off. (*points to cannonball*) That one gets the nod.

WESLEY: You wanted the brass.

ANNA: I've changed my mind. But we're going to
      haggle. If Bloom was giving me 50 percent off the
      waterbed, I don't see why I can't have the same
      on the cannonball.

WESLEY: We can still move this. It may go tomorrow.

ANNA: Give me a minute. (*pause*) You know, you
      really have to wonder at Council letting all those
      malls get built, don't you.

WESLEY: Council's preoccupied with growth. It's all
      they talk about. It was less than 1 percent last
      year. Now they want five. But who needs
      growth? If you want my opinion, the nation with
      a plummeting growth rate is making an impor-
      tant environmental contribution to the world.
      (*starting to orate*) If the human race is serious
      about surviving, I say we should be trying to
      *de*crease our economies, so we're using up less
      resources.

ANNA: Fewer.

WESLEY: Thank you Miss Eaton. Anyway, you know
      what I mean. Less is best. That's why Trudeau
      was such a fine statesman — he wrecked the
      economy.

ANNA: I doubt that was intentional.

WESLEY: Nevertheless. (*pause*) Anna — do you ever think you think too much?

ANNA: I'm usually too busy, and I'm not really of that bent. Deep down I'm pretty shallow. I used to kid myself in high school I was a thinker. I'd sit in the bleachers and ponder the nature of cheerleading.

WESLEY: No.

ANNA: Yes. I'd look at your sister bouncing up and down so earnestly and I'd try to figure why an intelligent girl like Jude would go in for all that tribal foofaraw.

WESLEY: Any conclusions?

ANNA: Tons. All those male hormones were being sweated out in violent endeavour on the field — there had to be a reason. Guys don't make mince-meat of each other for the good of their health, and one lousy trophy at the end of the season isn't much of an incentive, either. No, there had to be another reason and Jude and her squad of cheerleaders supplied it. I'd watch them wiggle and do the splits — and I understood. Football is symbolic foreplay.

WESLEY: Oh. Makes sense.

ANNA: And the pompoms. Have you ever noticed how cheerleaders grab 'em and shake 'em and hang onto the things for dear life, and all the while they look very, very happy? It's the high point of their lives because they've finally got total control over something important. Pompoms are symbolic testicles.

WESLEY: Oh my God.

ANNA: Told you I was shallow. One grade eleven textbook on tribal sociology and you just heard the sordid results. Naw, thinking stinks. I'm right off it. It's brought me nothing but heartache. I spent all of law school living with a two hundred pound lump of theory.

WESLEY: You've lost me.

ANNA: Albert. Albert Potter. He was a great guy but he theoried me to death. Albert couldn't stop thinking. He couldn't butter toast without pondering the significance of a knife wiping yellow stuff over a crispy surface.

WESLEY: You're making this up.

ANNA: Was the knife symbolic of society, rubbing a patina of civilization over something fundamentally inhospitable? And, if butter was civilization — what was jam?

WESLEY: Now I *know* you're making this up.

ANNA: I only wish.

WESLEY: Did Jason live with you and Albert?

ANNA: (*beat*) I couldn't afford it. (*slightly defensive*) I
    had to work part-time to put myself through, so
    Jace stayed here with Mom. She'd bus him down
    every weekend, or I'd come up. Actually, Jason
    was the clincher. Albert couldn't even feed Jason
    without trying to lure him into some discussion
    like "Why did dinosaurs go extinct" or "If you
    left a robot outside during a rainstorm, would the
    robot cry…"

WESLEY: Cry. How could you even tell?

ANNA: Don't you start. Aw, a kid can't have a theoreti-
    cal dad. I had to break it off. Three years down
    the tubes. Albert was really upset — and this was
    the shocker — "I'm not crying over you Anna,"
    he announces. "Don't flatter yourself. It's Jason
    I'm gonna miss." And Jason took it hard, too. I
    mean, I thought they lived on different planets
    but somehow they'd developed this bond. (*beat*)
    How on earth did I get on this!

WESLEY: You came in to buy a bed.

ANNA: And somehow we got got on to theory. My
    specialty.

WESLEY: It fascinates me. Probably because it's so
    foreign.

ANNA: I guess this place isn't exactly a philosopher's paradise.

WESLEY: God no. Your friend Albert'd make zilcho in commission up here. You've got to be pragmatic to sell beds. You think backs, bodies, wallets, comfort, coils — it doesn't require a whole lot of metaphysics.

ANNA: It's good to talk to an adult.

WESLEY: Yeah.

ANNA: You know, I almost wonder if a city this size isn't lonelier than a big one. Superficially it's friendlier here — but everyone seems so coupled. do you find that?

WESLEY: Yeah.

ANNA: It's like everyone in Ashburnham's lined up for the ark. They're all in twos and there aren't enough of us square pegs to form a queue in any other direction. But — "It's a great place to raise kids!"

BLOOM: Bloom to beds. Bloom to beds.

ANNA: I thought he went home —

WESLEY: (*intercom*) Yes sir.

BLOOM: I've finished the cash. It's under the you-know-what. Is that young lady still there?

WESLEY: She's still making up her mind.

BLOOM: She's not holding you hostage?

WESLEY: No sir.

BLOOM: I'd hate for us to get robbed our second last day.

WESLEY: I think we're safe.

BLOOM: I'm going then. Don't leave the stockroom light on this time.

WESLEY: No sir.

BLOOM: You forgot last night. It's a waste.

WESLEY: All shall be doused on the western front.

BLOOM: My son, will you ever talk normal? Still, I'm going to miss it. But I'm an old man, so now it's home I go. Good night. And good night customer.

ANNA: (*waves at intercom*) 'Night.

WESLEY: Shalom sir.

BLOOM: (*sighs*) O God our help in ages past.

WESLEY: Mazel Tov.

BLOOM: A-men brother.

WESLEY: Mr. Bloom.

BLOOM: I know.

BLOOM &
WESLEY: Next year in Jerusalem. (*hangs up mike*)

ANNA: That was interesting.

WESLEY: It's our good night routine. I act Jewish, he acts Protestant. It's for luck.

ANNA: Of course.

WESLEY: One night I wished him Mazel Tov and the next day we sold a colonial four poster that'd been sitting here for two years.

ANNA: So why does he talk Protestant?

WESLEY: It moves the velvet paintings.

ANNA: I don't know Wes —

WESLEY: — Not that anyone's religious. Actually, Bloom was, but they closed the synagogue on him. You have to have ten men, sort of like a quorum, and they were down to eight. And I used to go too — to church that is — I'm Presbyterian, but I quit. Five years ago. Jude still goes. It was hard for me to give up the concept of life after death. It meant I had to start going to the gym.

ANNA: I've followed everything up till that.

WESLEY: It was my theory that I'd come back in the next life, well, as a big stud. Like Billy, only with the ability to eat without scratching. It's a common theory of afterlife. You get reincarnated upwards: rooster to cow, cow to Wesley, Wesley to — big stud. So when I gave up religion I had to face the bitter truth: I wasn't ever going to reincarnate. I would never be a sex god in my next life. And, if I only had one life to live that meant I only had one body to live it in — I joined the Y the next day.

ANNA: It shows.

WESLEY: Huh?

ANNA: You look a lot better than you did in high school.

WESLEY: Bull.

ANNA: I'm not kidding. Your shoulders are really broad and —

WESLEY: — Stop it okay.

ANNA: I just said I thought you were looking —

WESLEY: — I heard you —

ANNA: — It was a compliment.

WESLEY: (*moving away*) Look. Do you want a bed? I'll sell you a bed.

ANNA: Ex-cuse me for living.

WESLEY: (*pause*) Sorry. I thought you were making fun of me.

ANNA: By saying you looked good? (*shakes head*)

WESLEY: Sorry. (*pause*) Why'd you come here?

ANNA: I smell a trick question. Because I want to buy a bed?

WESLEY: No, why'd you come back to Ashburnham? You didn't have to, so why did you?

ANNA: That's not very loyal to the town that bred and raised you.

WESLEY: I just mean you could've stayed in Toronto, there's lots of people there. Unmarried ones. Jude's always got a party or something on. You could've moved Jason down there.

ANNA: I didn't have a social life in Toronto, so I'm not losing anything by moving here. Mom's here and I think it's healthier in Ashburnham. If the kid and I had to make a go of it in Toronto we'd be locked away in some high-rise out in the suburbs and Jason'd be into God knows what. Which he's into here, no doubt, but on a more modest scale.

WESLEY: I still don't understand why you came back.

ANNA: Aw, I don't like sounding like the holy martyr all the time, but I'm here because Jason's here. I'm not uprooting him any more that I have to. He'll be finished high school in six years — if he wants to move then we will. But he's got to have roots somewhere and his, well, they're here.

WESLEY: But if the roots aren't good.

ANNA: I don't think I heard that. *Bad* roots?

WESLEY: I didn't mean bad, I meant not good. I mean, not good as in not-good-different, I think.

ANNA: You'd better explain.

WESLEY: I guess I mean I wonder if letting Jason have roots like you say is going to make up for well, him being denied a father.

ANNA: That's a neat little judgmental turd. I "denied" him a father?

WESLEY: I meant *life* denied him. Events. Same way I got gypped.

ANNA: And now it's "gypped."

WESLEY: I meant sort of —

ANNA: — I think you meant gypped. That's what you said.

WESLEY: That guy in law school — Albert — he would've married you.

ANNA: Oh. I'm supposed to get married so Jason can have a father.

WESLEY: You said Albert loved Jason. They had a bond. Do we have to talk about this —

ANNA: — I want to tell you something. People get married because they love each other, not because they happen to love the same third person.

WESLEY: You might have come to love Albert, in time.

ANNA: Not as a life partner. No.

WESLEY: But you're not sure.

ANNA: Of course I'm not sure. That's something you're never sure of.

WESLEY: Some people seem to know.

ANNA: What the living hell would you know. You're a goddamn Presbyterian nun! Look. I have been through hell and back for that son of mine. I've been through hell to become a lawyer, school, school, more school, articling, bar ads, part-time jobs and every extra minute, every free minute I had I came home and spent it with Jason. No matter how much I wanted to go out with my girlfriends, or out on a date…no matter how…

WESLEY: You didn't have to become a lawyer.

ANNA: You're right. I could've sold beds.

WESLEY: There's nothing wrong with selling beds.

ANNA: There's something wrong with hiding under them. I'm sorry, I'm having a real problem here. You can't stir your fanny out of this place to save your life but me, I'm supposed to forget any aspirations I might have — I'm supposed to marry some guy I don't love — what's the use. You're not the first one to say I've gypped him. Aren't you going to tell me I should've put him up for adoption? I get that thrown at me too. Well, you don't have the right. You just don't have the right. Not you, not this town, not anyone. Look at you. Where the hell do you get off judging me. I'd've thought that you, of all people, you, *Weirdley*, you'd be above that. You're pathetic. No sale. No sale. I'm history.

(ANNA *exits.* WESLEY *stands frozen, shocked*)

WESLEY: Anna. Anna. (*louder*) Anna! Wait! (*runs after her, to limit of doorway*) Anna! Don't go! (*runs to mike, speaks into it*) Anna! Anna! (*slams mike down*) Jesus. Jesus Christ, she's gone. (*runs to window, tries unsuccessfully to pull it so he can yell after her*) Get back here damnit! You can't walk out — open, come on, open — (*looks*) Where is she! Anna! Anna! (*now angry, directing it at objects as he returns to main part of room. He might rip diplomas off walls, kick pillows etc.*) Aw to hell with it, you're just like everybody else, so go to hell. Go to hell Anna Bregner! I hate you, I hate you all... I hate this place. (*pause*) I'm through. I'm through. No more Blooms, no more Bed Department, no more beds, no more goddamn swags, no more cannonball, no more brass... (*has reached desk, pulls out letter-opener, begins stalking waterbed*) So. So. No one wants you eh. You've been up here a little too long eh. Well it's time you earned your goddamn keep. Time we put you to good use. Maybe we'll just forget our little Midnight Madness Sale, maybe we'll have ourselves a Water Damage Sale! Time to die my undulating little friend. (*begins to raise letter opener*) Speak hands for me! (*pauses poised to stab, lowers*) Aw shit. (*sits on bed*) They never give me a chance. They never give me a goddamn chance... (*looks up to see* ANNA *, who has returned to the room*) Anna.

ANNA: (*coming over*) Are you okay?

WESLEY: You came back.

ANNA: Wes — are you —

WESLEY: Yes. No. I don't know. You came back, I thought you went.

ANNA: I never left. Are you *sure* you're okay? (*as* WESLEY *nods*) You sounded —

WESLEY: No, I was —

Andrew Lewarne as Wesley in the Lighthouse
Theatre production. Photo by Kevin Wood.

ANNA: — It's not a crime to get mad.

WESLEY: Sorry. (*beat*) Why am I apologizing? You stormed out of here and never let me finish what I was trying to say. We were having a good time and then whammo, out you go, and I'm all alone (*clicks fingers*) just like that, I'm alone. You have any idea what that's like?

ANNA: Yes.

WESLEY: No. No you don't, you don't have a clue, it's easy for you to run out of here, you've got some-place to run to. You've got people, your Mom, Jason... What have I got? I'll tell you what my life's like. When there's a symphony night I buy two tickets. I show up at the high school, they hand me my tickets and I shrug and say, "My friend's sick, I only need the one." So they won't know. I've only got one pillow on my bed — why would I ever expect a guest head? Some nights I lie there and look at the map I've got up on the wall beside my bed and I count all the dots that are cities and I wonder, "How many Wesleys are there in this goddamn country? How many oth-ers are lying there, alone, wondering what'd be like to have a real human being breathing beside them..." In the winter I don't shovel the walk. Why would I? The only ones using it are me, the neighbours' kids flogging chocolate bars, Jehovah's Witnesses. Winter progresses, there's just this one deepening groove, one person wide, one neat path to my door that I follow up and down, up and down, until thaw… One skinny little path…

ANNA: I understand.

WESLEY: How could you!

ANNA: There's more that one kind of lonely. You've got one kind, I've got another. I've got a family but I don't have anyone — to talk to — you know — like an adult, a friend…. So what do I do with the first one I meet? I blow my stack. I got downstairs — oh I just feel sick about what I said, Wes, I'm truly sorry.

WESLEY: For what?

ANNA: Come on, for being a witch, for saying —

WESLEY: — Everything you said was true. I *am* pathetic. That was a good word. You must take me for the biggest idiot in the world.

ANNA: That's not what I think at all.

WESLEY: I can never say what I'm thinking. Not when it's important. I want to do something or say something and it just doesn't come out. I wanted to tell you I admire you. For coming back here, for facing everyone, for never letting things get you down, or screw you up, for being so brave.

Andrew Lewarne as Wesley and Jacquie Presly as Anna in the Lighthouse Theatre production. Photo by Kevin Wood.

ANNA: That's a laugh.

WESLEY: You've raised a son on your own and done it well. That's brave. I could never have done that!

ANNA: Who says I've done it well. I've been an absentee parent. Sure — Jason's a good kid — right now — but what's to stop him becoming a mess later? I don't know if I've — I've been around him enough to instil any values —

WESLEY: — Sure you have —

ANNA: — Enough to keep him out of trouble? Don't admire me for being a successful parent. The jury's still out on that one. And I'm not brave. I'm terrified. I don't know if the kid and I can get it together and he's all I've got. Jason is it. No, I'm not brave… (*touches* WESLEY, *a smile*) We have a lot in common, you and I. We're both lonely, we're both scared. Maybe it is harder for you. You live alone, you work here alone. And this place, this room, it's kind of a time warp. I don't mean that negatively, just that —

WESLEY: It's only one more day.

ANNA: But all those years.

WESLEY: I chose it. At least I think I chose it. You make your bed…

ANNA: The last time I was up here, it was with Dan. Nothing's changed in fourteen years. Well — you're here. Dan was Jason's father. We weren't actually looking for a bed; that would've been politically incorrect. Just a mattress. Who was selling up here then?

WESLEY: Probably Mr. Bishop. Tall, gaunt?

ANNA: Ichabod Cranish.

WESLEY: (*a laugh*) Yes. That's him.

ANNA: He looked at us pretty dimly. I was seventeen. Maybe he was just being sniffy because we only wanted a mattress, but Dan thought he was laying a morality trip on us.

WESLEY: Maybe Bishop was jealous.

ANNA: You think so?

WESLEY: I get that way. Everyone who comes up here is happy. People buy beds for happy reasons — they're setting up house or they've just moved in with someone or they've worn out their old bed. People like coming to bed departments.

ANNA: What about people with bad backs?

WESLEY: I sell them orthopaedic mattresses.

ANNA: Well there you go.

WESLEY: Do you — do you like sherry?

ANNA: Hate it. Why.

WESLEY: I — I sometimes have a glass after closing.

ANNA: How posh. Go ahead — don't let me stop you.

WESLEY: (*producing two styrofoam cups*) You know, you haven't lived till you've tasted sherry out of styrofoam.

ANNA: Twist my arm. I don't suppose you've got some pretzels. I missed dinner.

WESLEY: Chocolate-topped digestives.

ANNA: With sherry?

WESLEY: It's an acquired taste.

ANNA: Let's give her a shot.

WESLEY: I used to have a Coke after closing with Mr. Hamilton, when he ran Lighting. After he retired, I upped the ante.

ANNA: This isn't so bad.

WESLEY: It's good stuff. I don't have a lot of indulgences, but this, and the digestives, are two.

ANNA: Wes. (*holds up cup*) Cheers big guy. (WESLEY *holds up his cup; they "clink"*) You know, it was all your sister's fault I even met Dan.

Michelle Fisk as Anna in the Tarragon Theatre production.
Photo by Michael Cooper.

WESLEY: Why?

ANNA: Jude and I made a pact to get stoned on her seventeenth birthday, so we went down to War Memorial Park to buy dope. Jude didn't want to get it at school because she was a cheerleader and — nice girls didn't smoke pot.

WESLEY: Sounds like a book title.

ANNA: We went down to the park one night but your big bold sister chickened out so I went in alone.

WESLEY: Weren't you scared?

ANNA: Petrified. I asked the first hippie I met for a "nickel bag". I knew that much — it's five bucks worth. And then — I kind of just stayed there, in the park. It was barely spring but it was full of people — somebody was sitting on the steps of the statue, tapping a tambourine. There were little circles of people sitting around, talking, smoking up — in downtown Ashburnham! And that's when I met Dan. He was wearing an Indian shirt, beads, the whole number, bare feet… He wasn't a bit like any of the guys at school. He had these gentle, wicked eyes — woof, I was a goner. (*pause, a bit self-conscious, a little laugh*) See — this is how you can tell *I'm* lonely — I'm rambling on like a leaky faucet. But as I said — it's good to talk to an adult. Just make sure this stays out of the scrapbook.

WESLEY: It'll cost you a bed.

ANNA: (*indicating waterbed*) Not the...

(WESLEY *nods*)

ANNA: You're a cruel man, Wesley Marshall. (*pause*) So anyway, I hung out at that park a lot over the next few months. Somehow I became "Dan's woman" — this was pre-feminism, remember. It was pretty weird for a high school girl. I was going steady and I didn't even know it. I suppose I could've guessed — Dan always passed me the joint first.

WESLEY: Your mother must have been going nuts.

ANNA: She was working crazy hours at the hospital — she never knew.

WESLEY: I don't understand why you'd pick Dan. Why not a football hero?

ANNA: Dan was a lot more exciting than anyone at Ashburnham High. And it wasn't only him — there was a group of new people, new music, poetry. Dan wrote poetry. Can you imagine Billy writing a poem? Dan was a sociology major — theories galore. You know me and theoretical men. He had ideas about society and education and an endless supply of ideas about sex. That's another thing about Dan — he was the first guy

who didn't treat me like I was inventory. Billy —
he was next thing to a rapist, an octopus. With
Dan I was getting respect and no pressure. You
know, I look at Jace and I pray to God he never
turns into one of those high school hornballs. I've
got to teach him girls aren't for pawing.

WESLEY: Good luck.

ANNA: You didn't paw.

WESLEY: I didn't date. I wanted to, I just didn't know
how to set the whole process in motion.

ANNA: You want the truth? Jude asked me if she could
ask you to ask me to the grade twelve prom.

WESLEY: Jeez. That would've been some disaster. I
didn't even know how to dance. You'd have been
embarrassed.

ANNA: Hell. I'd have got us stoned out of our gourds.
That would've given them something to talk
about. You in a tux, me in chiffon, floating down
the receiving line. Good evening Principal
Wilson. And hey — Mrs. Wilson. Groovy dress
Miss Eaton.

WESLEY: (*having fun*) Like hey man, Anna, it's like
Camelot man.

(*Shared laugh*)

ANNA: You're right. It wouldn't have worked. So —
    you have any other indulgences?

WESLEY: Not really. I read like a maniac.

ANNA: Me too, when I have time. I'm fighting my way
    through Faulkner.

WESLEY: I love Faulkner! Which one are you reading?

ANNA: *Absolam, Absolam!*

    (*They groan*)

    I know. (*southern accent*) It's tough sleddin suh.
    But uh truh, uh truh. Dan was a big Faulkner fan
    too. He used to sit in the park and read his brains
    out. First he'd smoke 'em out, then he'd read 'em
    out. He told me he could read *Ulysses* stoned.

WESLEY: You can't even read it unstoned! Jeez — if I'd
    known you could *read* in that park —

ANNA: You could do anything there.

WESLEY: I can't recall seeing anyone reading. I had to
    walk through there on the way home from the
    library and I'm sorry — I don't remember seeing
    books. Do you know how hard it was walking by
    those people — when you know you're being
    watched and you're trying to walk normal but
    your knees lock, your bum petrifies...

ANNA: Can you imagine if you'd ever stopped and had a toke?

WESLEY: The gap between the sidewalk and the park benches wasn't for me to cross.

ANNA: It was a very accepting time.

WESLEY: In retrospect.

ANNA: I was there. It was different, and that's not just rose-coloured glasses.

WESLEY: Then why didn't it last?

ANNA: It was too gentle. We had to turn our backs on it for self-preservation. But it's still in me. I'm waiting. One of these days Jupiter and Mars are going to realign — and Anna Bregner will be ready.

WESLEY: You're a lawyer!

ANNA: I'll cover my briefcase in flower decals. (*holds out cup*)

WESLEY: More?

ANNA: Why not.

WESLEY: (*pouring*) Where's Dan now?

ANNA: Out west, running a group home. He'd be great at it. When I met him he was manager of the Y Drop-in Centre.

WESLEY: I never went.

ANNA: No one from our school did.

WESLEY: Didn't you have to be on a bad trip?

ANNA: That was the Crisis Centre. We were just drop-in. We played music, had non-competitive sports, did crafts. (*covers face with hands*) Talk about another era! I can't imagine Jason and his buddies getting into beadwork!

WESLEY: I was never any good at crafts but I liked gardening.

ANNA: That was politically correct — you'd've fit right in.

WESLEY: Roses.

ANNA: (*shaking head*) It had to be veggies or dope. Do you remember Magic Meadows? We were the organizers. The name was my idea.

WESLEY: Mom fought that thing like crazy.

ANNA: All the neighbours did.

WESLEY: She was convinced there'd be a mass orgy up there and we'd have drug-crazed hippies spilling into our backyard, doing rude things to her rose-bushes.

ANNA: (*laughs*) All that opposition made it hell to organize. We had to build outhouses because nobody'd rent them to us. We had a hassle-free first aid tent and a volunteer clean-up crew. There was a vegetarian kitchen —

WESLEY: — And the music. Whew.

ANNA: Yeah.

WESLEY: We could hear it down the hill. All over the city, for that matter.

ANNA: We'd booked the biggies: Major Hooples, Little Caesar, Mandala.

WESLEY: I snuck up the hill and watched from the trees.

ANNA: You should've joined us.

WESLEY: After the crusading Mom did, I'd have felt like Benedict Arnold. I'm sure she had the festival under surveillance. She probably had her bridge club in disguise, slipping through the crowds taking photos with their Brownies.

ANNA: (*laughs*) It was an incredible day. It really worked. It was so peaceful, so unlike anything we'd ever had here.

WESLEY: Mom was really disappointed nothing evil happened.

ANNA: — We showed 'em. We ended it exactly at nightfall, as ordered by Council. The cleanup brigade was too stoned, so Dan and I ended up raking the lawns and bagging everything. I didn't care. I was so happy — I belonged. I went home with Dan that night and for the first time I stayed over. I didn't care anymore. Things had been so good, I just felt immune. Dan lived in one of those big student houses near the cathedral, on Fleming Place. He had the whole top floor, it was the attic really, but he'd fixed it up. There was a balcony with doors that opened. Our mattress was right there, so we were half outside. If it rained it'd get damp —

WESLEY: — Oh jeez, I can't condone bed abuse.

ANNA: A half hour ago you were all set to murder one. You'll be relieved to know we eventually got wise and put up a little awning. And there was a Manitoba maple growing up the front of the house — its leaves were like a curtain and that was wonderful in the mornings because the sun would come through. Or, if there was a moon, there'd be a back glow...

WESLEY: It sounds nice.

ANNA: Yeah. It rained finally that night. We woke about four or five, to the drumming on the roof. And there were pigeons in the eaves, they made pigeon noises which actually kind of sound like

you know, people making love, which might
have given us the idea... (*embarrassed now, a bit*)
Anyway, we did — make love — and Jason got
the nod. That was the night, I'm sure that was the
night. (*pause*) Do you understand about my boy
now?

WESLEY: I think so.

ANNA: That summer with Dan was the first time in my
life — it was the only time — when I just threw
up my hands and said, "Let the chips fall where
they may, I'm going with the flow." Remember
that expression? Jason was conceived in the very
best night of my best summer, with a man I loved
— so I have to ask you Wes, how many kids get a
head-start like that?

WESLEY: I'm glad you've told me all this. I — we all
tend to be — *I* can be judgmental. You heard me
earlier. My sister would've had you in New York
in ten minutes flat.

ANNA: Having an abortion? Mom and I discussed it,
but, I don't know, I guess it's one of those things I
can accept for other people but not for me. And
you know, there's hardly a day goes by that I
don't thank God I kept him. Even when I'm dead
tired and he's pissing me off. Which is often.
Anyway, the rest is history. I started grade thir-

teen but, by October, I knew the jig was up and
school seemed a bit irrelevant. I was still with
Dan. You can't imagine how weird it is being
pregnant in high school. I'd be in the girls' can
and hear them talking about sex — some were
speculating; others were having sex but not fun
and, well, I was having both. I didn't have to
worry about getting pregnant anymore and, with
that load off my shoulders — well! School activi-
ties seemed really dumb. *Everything* seemed
dumb. (*pause*) Inevitably, the names started. Do
you remember what they called me?

WESLEY: Yes.

ANNA: I don't know how they found out so fast. I
wasn't showing.

WESLEY: You only had to tell one person.

ANNA: Mary Lou Winters.

WESLEY: Who told my sister. Who told Billy. The minute news like that crosses to the other sex —

ANNA: Pincushion. Pincushion Bregner. If it didn't
represent so much loathing, it'd almost be funny.

WESLEY: It could never be funny.

ANNA: At the start I was never too sure what I was
hearing — it'd be a loud whisper at the back of

the class (*loud whisper*) "Pincushion" — then giggles. Snickers. I'd catch people's eyes flickering down to my stomach, real fast, then up again. Mary Lou and your sister and everyone else stopped walking with me between classes. What, did they think they could catch it? Aw, I should've just quit but Mom wanted me to go as long as possible. Then, one morning in December, about three weeks before Christmas, I opened my locker and there were condoms draped over my books. A half dozen. They looked used, it was probably just spit, it doesn't matter... it was the hatred behind it.

WESLEY: I knew all this.

ANNA: I stood in front of my locker. I just stood there, staring. I didn't know what to do. I felt ashamed, grossed out — then angry. Really angry. I couldn't touch them and I wasn't going to remove them, not with everyone hanging about — and I didn't know how many were in on it but not a damn one of them was going to have the satisfaction of watching me clean my locker. So I marched down to see Vice Principal Whatshisname —

WESLEY: — Tomlinson —

ANNA: — He already knew I was pregnant. How the hell *he* found out, I'll never know. I said, "Sir, there are some things in my locker I want removed and I'm not doing it." I told him point blank what they were.

WESLEY: And then you got the word.

ANNA: How'd you know all this.

WESLEY: The usual route. Mary Lou, to Jude, to me.

ANNA: *I* was the one to be removed. Plus, it had to happen before I started showing. I had to leave at Christmas. Three weeks notice. I could write my mid-terms, then out. And furthermore, I was responsible for the sanctity of my locker. (*pause*) I waited until everyone was in class, then I went back upstairs. I put on my gloves, I removed the safes, scrubbed the locker, went to the can, and I was sick. I cried. I locked myself in a cubicle and cried my guts out. Then I dried my tears, I threw out the gloves, I went and got a late slip from that Tomlinson — goof — and I marched into class.

WESLEY: It's so unfair they made you leave.

ANNA: I doubt I could've taken another six months of whispers. I'm honestly not tough enough.

WESLEY: We're a union of two on that. (*pause*) I thought of you as — as Pincushion too.

ANNA: Do you now?

WESLEY: Of course not. But I sure did then.

ANNA: Why should you have been any different?

WESLEY: I should've known better.

ANNA: Ah, it's ancient history now. It's funny how much I still care though. God, half an hour ago I stomped out of here and all you'd said was —

WESLEY: —I'd said enough. (*pause*) It was Billy who stuffed your locker.

ANNA: That's no surprise.

WESLEY: I overheard him tell Jude. The night before. Jude didn't agree but she didn't try and stop him. I didn't think it was right either, but mostly I was grateful that for once they weren't doing anything to me. We're a very imperfect species. (*holds up bottle*) A little more?

ANNA: Oh I'd better go.

WESLEY: No. That is, not unless you want to.

ANNA: I'd like to stay —

WESLEY: — You shouldn't let me drink alone.

ANNA: Half a glass then. (*as* WESLEY *pours*) A bit more than that, chintzbag.

WESLEY: You said half.

ANNA: I like my halves closer to full. Shoot me a digestive. If I throw back enough of this hooch it may drown out my son the human chain saw. Maybe I'll fall asleep quickly for a change.

WESLEY: I count sheep.

ANNA: Never worked for me.

WESLEY: I count sheep, then I recite the prime ministers in chronological order. I have a big map of Canada beside my bed — it stretches across the entire wall — and I look at it and mentally drive across the country.

ANNA: Which province do you sleep in?

WESLEY: Huh?

ANNA: If the map stretches the length of your bed —

WESLEY: Oh, Nova Scotia. I lay my head just outside Halifax. I tried sleeping under Vancouver but I kept getting these really bizarre dreams. (*pause*) If the map thing doesn't work, I just lie there and watch the moon. I love it when the moon's full and a cloud passes in front of it. (*smile*) I lie back and howl. (*quieter*) Some nights I put myself to sleep thinking about suicide. About how I'd do it and who'd find me and after how long, then how the world will take the news. Will I get a little notice in the *Examiner*, will the neighbours have a wake — they'd better after all the raffle tickets their kids have sold me.

ANNA: What a sad way to make yourself fall asleep.

WESLEY: Oh I'd never do it, don't get me wrong. It's just a device.

ANNA: Next time you're compiling the list of mourners, add me.

WESLEY: You'll come?

ANNA: I'll even help Jude with the arrangements. I'll lay in the sherry and the memorial digestives.

WESLEY: Spare no expense.

ANNA: Jace can pass food. We can have a short homily from Mary Lou Slutbrain Winters. But Wes: poor Mr. Bloom will want to know why.

WESLEY: Tell him the truth. "Sir: it was the waterbed. It was an emotional albatross." (*pause*) I'm glad you came tonight.

ANNA: I did consider going to Nutty Normans. Something kind of drew me here. Kismet maybe. Wes. Tell me if I'm out of line. (*pause*) I saw the assembly.

WESLEY: I wondered when that would come up.

ANNA: I've thought of it, of you, actually, through the years.

Kate Hurman as Anna and Mo Bock as Wesley in the Thousand Islands Playhouse production at the Upper Canada Playhouse. Photo by Dan Pritchard.

WESLEY: (*starting to close up*) I've never talked to anyone about it.

ANNA: Not even Jude?

WESLEY: Never. It was too — humiliating.

ANNA: Not even the day it happened?

WESLEY: Jude came home late that night and went to bed without speaking to me. I was waiting up, praying to God she'd knock on my door and tell me it wasn't as bad — as bad as I knew it was. She didn't knock. The next day it was too late. I'd lain awake all night wondering what the hell I could do to save myself and, by the time dawn rolled around I knew I couldn't go back to school. Ever. I was done. Kaputski.

ANNA: Why did you do it!

WESLEY: They promised me I could join the Cougars Club.

ANNA: Who — Billy?

WESLEY: All of them. They said if I did my thing at the Christmas assembly nobody would blackball me.

ANNA: Why would you even want to belong to a club like that?

WESLEY: Look. If some one offers you acceptance you don't argue. I wanted to belong. To anything! I'd waited seventeen, eighteen years for it — it was full steam ahead, damn the torpedoes... They said I'd knock them dead. I got my toga — it was actually a flannelette sheet I'd smuggled past Mom that morning — and I changed in the dressing room and waited at the door to the gym. The cheerleaders were doing the skit before me; I stood in line behind them — they didn't really look at me, why would they? Then they ran out and did their thing and it was my turn... Billy got up to the mike and announced me. (*pause*) When he said he'd located the madman of ancient Rome, the love god of grade thirteen Latin...I knew.

ANNA: It was a set-up.

WESLEY: I'd fallen for it. But it was too late.

ANNA: Why did you go out!

WESLEY: I had no choice...

ANNA: I remember how quiet it got.

WESLEY: It's always like that before a sacrifice.

ANNA: You looked so scared. And your arms were so white...

WESLEY: My legs were trembling so much it was like walking on sticks of Jello. I went over to the mike and unscrewed it. That was some feat with my hand going like this. (holds up hand, makes it shake) And then I started. (*recites*)

"The skies are painted with unnumbered sparks,
They were all fire, and every one doth shine;
But there's but one in all doth hold his place.
So in the world: 'tis furnished well with men,
And men are flesh and blood..."

I've run it through my head a million times. But this is where it started. Just a few at first.

"Yet in the number I do know but one
That unassailable holds on his rank..."

They were chanting by now.

ANNA: Why didn't you stop!

WESLEY: I should've but I thought...I don't know, I thought that maybe when I did the death part, when I died, that would satisfy them, maybe all they wanted was some histrionics...

"Doth not Brutus bootless kneel?

Speak hands for me!"

(*mimes being stabbed*) I was drowned out by now, even with the mike. It was coming from every corner of that gym — from the front row of the bleachers where the seniors were, right up to the rafters, way back, from the younger grades and from the ones peering in from the hall — they were all shouting, it was hate, Anna, it had to have been, and I was like a lightning rod for it; I stood there and attracted hate and, when I fell to the floor, it was like a mighty wave, a mighty wave of ridicule that washed over me, all those voices, a thousand people yelling *Weirdley*. Weirdley. My label. The name I'd been called right from the first day I'd set foot in that school and the name I thought I was going to leave behind that afternoon. (*pause*) I lay there on the gym floor, in front of them all — I wanted to die — I wanted to die right then and there —

ANNA: (*touching him*) Wesley —

WESLEY: (*accepts touch*) I'm OK. (*pause*) I wasn't sure the legs were even going to get me up and out of there, but they did, I managed to stumble away. I ran home, it was like I could hear the chanting all the way back, right into the house. It followed me upstairs, up into my room and I couldn't shut it out until I'd crawled into bed and pulled my covers and my pillow over my head. Then, finally, it started going away.

ANNA: I yelled it too.

WESLEY: (*smiling, quietly*) Et tu Brute? (*pause*) Of course you did. Why wouldn't you have?

ANNA: Pincushion, of all people, should've known better.

WESLEY: You were only one voice in a thousand.

ANNA: Can you ever forgive me?

WESLEY: Of course.

ANNA: Do you forgive them?

WESLEY: I pretty much have to.

ANNA: Where do you suppose it all stops?

WESLEY: The name-calling? I doubt it ever does. It gets subtler with adults.

ANNA: Or maybe we just pass it down to the next generation. I meant to get down here at nine tonight. Ten at the latest. But Jason was hanging about the apartment after supper and then he dragged off to bed early. I knew something was bugging him. I went and sat on his bed and asked him. He tried to be the big tough guy for a minute but I kept on his case and finally he burst into tears. He let me hug him — he *never* lets me do that anymore — and then he told me the kids at school are making fun of him for never having had a father. They're calling him "bastard".

WESLEY: Oh nice.

ANNA: Somewhere it has to end.

WESLEY: I think I'd rather be called bastard than Weirdley.

ANNA: Tell that to Jason.

WESLEY: I guess Weirdley'd sound pretty good to him right now.

ANNA: He's tough. It'll blow over. I just hope he never comes to hate me for it.

WESLEY: (*a smile*) You're tough. It'll blow over.

ANNA: I hope so. (*pause*) The bed.

WESLEY: It's yours. Fifty percent off.

(ANNA *gives a triumphant cheer*)

It'll be delivered tomorrow.

ANNA: I could squeeze it in the car.

WESLEY: Not the mattress. And you can't drive around town at midnight with a mattress tied to your roof.

ANNA: People might get the wrong impression.

WESLEY: (*mock announcing*) Pincushion makes house calls!

ANNA: Why don't I come back tomorrow and we'll load it then. I'll bring Jason — you can meet him. Though I probably shouldn't let him see this waterbed.

WESLEY: There's still a bit of sherry left, I think. (*produces a full bottle*)

ANNA: (*laughs*) If I have any more of that stuff I'm liable to start buying art.

WESLEY: "Stag in a Glen"?

ANNA: Anything, so long as it's on velvet.

WESLEY: Protestant.

ANNA: I could use something for my office, wherever that'll be. God. That's a whole 'nuther hassle.

WESLEY: After tomorrow you can have this place.

ANNA: I'm leaning towards a mall, if you want the dirty truth. I could run a regular practice by day and on Thursday evenings have a clinic. For kids. They hang out there. It's the teenage girls I worry about. They need someone to tell them their rights — who better than me?

WESLEY: You really are something.

ANNA: You can say that because you haven't seen enough of me yet. (*pause*) So. What about you?

WESLEY: What about me? Who knows. You need a receptionist?

ANNA: You must have some idea what you're going to do.

WESLEY: Not the foggiest. I never had to think much about the future. I didn't expect to be here forever — I knew this wasn't permanent. But the future? Anna: in just a few hours I'm starting something new. The day after tomorrow I'll wake up and look at the map beside my bed and know I don't have to drive across Canada just in my mind anymore. I can do it for real. And I can take as long as I damn well want. Or I can stay home and do nothing. Or go out and look for a job. Am I ready for the future? Of course not, who ever is. But — but I think that maybe for the first time in my life — I'm going to toss the cat a doughnut.

ANNA: I beg your pardon.

WESLEY: Go with the flow, to use your expression.

ANNA: You may wash up in some funny places.

WESLEY: Not me — I don't flow nowhere fast.

ANNA: (*pause*) You may fall in love.

WESLEY: It's an option.

ANNA: Some call it an imperative.

WESLEY: Not when it's never happened. I sell the catalysts of it — that's as close as I get.

ANNA: But you've dated.

WESLEY: (*rueful smile*) Poorly. The woman who worked here in Accounting asked me out on a picnic and I took folding chairs. There've been others — they just don't work out. I've never — I've never been in love. Never. (*pause*) What's it like!

ANNA: It's terrifying. It's like taking a long deep breath and suddenly you know you can't stop inhaling. You kind of want to stop and you kind of don't but it doesn't matter anyway because you can't — you keep inhaling, you think you're going to burst and you just keep getting bigger and bigger.

WESLEY: I'm so sick of being lonely.

ANNA: Good.

WESLEY: I want to —

ANNA: — You will —

WESLEY: — You think?

ANNA: You know how you were talking about how every winter there's just one narrow path to your door. (*beat*) Things may change next winter.

WESLEY: How's that?

ANNA: (*pause*) One day you might look out your bedroom window and see a woman walking up that path.

WESLEY: My sister.

ANNA: No.

WESLEY: An Avon lady wasting her time.

ANNA: It's night. It's a woman about your age, nicely dressed, a little brassy on the outside —

WESLEY: Is this theoretical?

ANNA: (*getting courage*) You're upstairs. You think there's a mistake or something, maybe the woman was an apparition, so you go back to bed. However the woman has very definitely arrived at your side door. She walks in — I guess you forgot to lock up — you hear the door slam and then she stamps her feet on the kitchen mat.

WESLEY: Do you mind if she leaves her shoes in the sunporch?

ANNA: It's too cold for that. And she's in a bit of a hurry because even though she's a modern woman — a woman of the 90s almost — she's losing her nerve. Fast.

WESLEY: Would it help her if the lights were left on?

ANNA: Just the hall one.

WESLEY: There's a night light at the top of the stairs.

ANNA: Perfect.

WESLEY: What if I'm at the head of the staircase, challenging this intruder.

ANNA: Not tonight. Tonight you're going with the flow.

WESLEY: I'm scared then.

ANNA: This woman walks up the stairs — do they creak?

WESLEY: Like crazy.

ANNA: She creaks up the stairs and goes straight to your bedroom.

WESLEY: There's four doors to chose from. How'd she know the right room?

ANNA: It's the one with the map. She walks into the bedroom and, for one moment, you see her silhouetted in the faint glow of your nightlight. Perhaps a stray bit of moonlight plays across her face.

WESLEY: (*understanding*) I think she'd be beautiful in moonlight.

ANNA: (*pause*) She takes off her coat and her shoes, then everything else, and she walks quickly over the cold linoleum — am I right, it's linoleum?

(WESLEY *nods*)

She walks over to where you're lying on your bed, with your head under Halifax, and your toes sticking up near Vancouver, and…

John Dolan as Wesley and Michelle Fisk as Anna in the Tarragon Theatre production. Photo by Michael Cooper.

WESLEY: And what? What does she do?

ANNA: She drops in on Winnipeg.

(ANNA *and* WESLEY *both laugh*)

(*slapping self in mock shock*) What a pincushion!

WESLEY: (*pause*) Who in her right mind would want to visit Winnipeg in the dead of winter?

ANNA: You'd be surprised.

WESLEY: I can't believe this.

ANNA: It comes from tossing cats doughnuts.

WESLEY: (*after a pause*) Anna. I have to close up. I have to make sure Mr. Bloom put the cash in the right place and then I have to set the burglar alarms and if I'm really brave I'll go check and make sure nobody's hiding out in the basement. You can't mess around with theory forever, not when you have a store to close.

ANNA: I was afraid not.

WESLEY: You have to be practical.

ANNA: I guess.

WESLEY: (*pause*) And what would be most practical is if we went back to our respective homes and got ourselves good nights' sleeps. Really good sleeps. In fact, I suggest you sleep in as late as you can. Tomorrow, treat yourself to a day on the town. Don't paint or wallpaper. Hang out at a shopping mall with Jason. Take him for a hamburger. Have a candlelight dinner at home with your Mom.

ANNA: Thanks for the thrilling itinerary.

WESLEY: I'm not finished. After dinner, watch some TV with Jason. Put on a nice dress. Your best dress, actually, then cool your heels until 9:30.

ANNA: And then?

WESLEY: And then get in your car and drive down to Bloom's Furniture. There's going to be a party.

ANNA: A real party?

WESLEY: You can't party in theory. And sometimes it's — it's — sometimes it's nice to have a date.

ANNA: Sometimes it's nice to be one.

WESLEY: After that...

ANNA: After that?

WESLEY: I don't know what happens.

ANNA: I guess we go with the flow.

WESLEY: It'll be a slow flow.

ANNA: Maybe like taking a long deep breath and
    never knowing where it'll end.

WESLEY: Yes. That's exactly what it'll be like.

> *Black.*
>
> *The End*

Memories of You

Wendy Lill

The life of Elizabeth Smart pivoted on a
turbulent affair that produced one book and four
children. When her youngest daughter, the
resentful and drug-ridden Rose comes to visit, an
explosion of emotion between mother and
daughter erupts, as well as an explosion of
memories for Smart.

*Memories is beautifully written… Everything about
it reaches for the ecstatic — its pleasure, its sensuality
and its pain. Memories is a courageous and
profoundly moving play…*

ROBERT ENRIGHT, CBC RADIO